MW01716264

Enjoy!

To my friend, Carolyn.

Virginia Elaine Sievers

WAITING

A Collective

by

Virginia Sievers

3rd Edition

ISBN-13:
978-0692466117 (Virginia Sievers)

ISBN-10:
0692466118

This book is a work of fiction. Names, characters, places, and incidents either are the product of the author's imagination or are used fictitiously. Any resemblance to actual events or locales or persons, living or dead, is entirely coincidental.

All You Can Eat Books

Chanhassen, Minnesota

Honors for "Waiting: a Collective"

Awards

"Waiting: a Collective", in its original form was awarded *Honorable Mention for Published Fiction* in the Arizona Literary Writer's Contest for 2014.

The first story, **"Waiting"**, in its original form was awarded *First Prize for Short Story* in the 2013 Contest.

Comments

"Waiting: a Collective" has a readers' five-star average rating on Amazon.com. Some of the offerings of praise are:

Heartwarming and Most Meaningful

Most meaningful is an understatement! This book is a must read for all of us approaching advanced years. Very highly recommended.

Very Insightful

A wonderful book that provides a glimpse into the lives of older people, and does it in a way that has them seem very human. It's a very insightful book, providing a view of these people as we don't ever get to see them.

Great Read

I loved how the stories were intertwined and connected together. The storytelling was fantastic. I often felt touched by the characters' situations. I would recommend this book.

Great Book

Very good book to get you to think about what is really important in life and who we could give support to in our neighborhood.

A Different Perspective

A book for seniors and anyone else who knows or loves one. Provides sensitive insight into the realities of aging.

---

about the Collective . . .

Amanda, Marty, Agnes, Ann and Matthew, and Rose wait for their appointments in a busy doctor's office. They are people we know. They are our friends, our parents, and our co-workers. They are people who are old.

As they confront keen issues, waiting affords time for reflection and observation and, sometimes, for action.

This is a small Collective within a large Collective; that of the elderly. As the elderly come to terms with issues of aging, they are worthy of admiration and reverence.

The Collective

Amanda Riperos

Marty Jasper

Agnes Bruninski

Ann and Matthew Jordan

Rose Middleton

Amanda Riperos

"We shall all die, and our lives will be irrelevant then."

Jeanette Winterson

Waiting

My name is Amanda Riperos, and I am an old person.

In this waiting room we are all old people, sitting quietly on our chairs and marking time together. Some of us leaf through magazines. Some of us have our eyes on the wall television where the volume is turned low. On the screen a smiling blonde talks to us, peppering her talk with inane little laughs as she tells us about a popular and trendy restaurant we should visit. Some of us close our eyes and doze. I am reading a magazine but I put it down and pick up a newspaper another person has left behind.

When the nurse opens the inner door and walks briskly toward us we look up expectantly. She walks with authority and she looks cross, almost currish. Checking a green file, she struggles to pronounce a name while her eyes impatiently scan the room. A woman nods, gets up slowly from her chair, makes her way to the door and, on the way, tells the nurse how the name should be pronounced. *"Broo nin' ski,"* she says, "not Brou nis' ki." The nurse narrows her eyes and openly frowns at the woman. She doesn't acknowledge the correction. I watch from my chair and think this nurse is rude and insensitive and I wonder if she is controlling. I wonder if she is a *Nurse Ratched* kind of person.

Sitting beside me an overweight and ill-kept man sighs when his name is not called. He is restless. Unlike most of us, he wants to talk.

"Have you been here long?" he asks.

"Yes, for some time," I reply. The man already knows this.

"I've been here for an hour," he tells me. "It's busy today." He nervously shifts his body in the chair.

"Yes," I agree. I don't extend the conversation. Hopefully, he won't go on with his talk.

Across the room a quiet couple listens. As they sit close, they hold hands. The man looks at his watch and points to it. The woman, eyes twinkling, nods her head as she points to her watch, too. They look at each other knowingly and break into smiles. I watch them with disdain, resenting their closeness and resenting their happiness and I think their private joke is silly. My face is in a frown but I remember that our nurse, our own *Nurse Ratched*, is a frowner and her frown doesn't become her. I quickly erase mine and purposely look away.

When I scan the headlines in the newspaper there is nothing that interests me. As It slips to my lap my hands idly play with the loose pages.

The outside door opens. A new couple comes into the room. As her partner watches the woman struggles to maneuver her walker through the door. She gets it inside and they both head for two chairs near the check-in counter. The man stops at the counter to write on the patient clipboard and I see that, while he is writing, the woman's eyes fill with tears. Sitting down carefully on one of the chairs she puts her purse on her walker and tries to brush away the tears but they slide down her cheeks. Seeing the tears makes me sad for the woman. I want to walk across the room to offer comfort but, once again, I purposely look away.

Nurse Ratched is back, clutching a red file this time. Her eyes narrow. In her impatient voice she calls out a name. The restless man who waited for an hour gets up quickly and walks fast as he follows the nurse through her door. "Finally," he says loudly.

I try reading the newspaper again, then sit quietly for a long time with the paper on my lap. I am tired but make an effort to sit up tall and straight. Someone turned the television off so the loud steady ticking of the wall clock fills the quiet space.

The inner door opens. "Riperos," Nurse Ratched calls into the quiet as she comes into the room. I don't bother to correct the mispronunciation of my name. I just stand and follow her to the door, walking as fast as I can manage. At best, though, my fast walk is a slow dragging shuffle; a shuffle I own now. Lately it has become an embarrassment. To compensate for my slowness I hold my head high and focus my eyes straight ahead.

It is a struggle to keep up with Nurse Ratched's fast pace. Even though my feet slowly drag, my mind is on fast forward. Hurting truths rush into my head.

I consider them one-by-one.

"So it all comes to this," I think. It all comes to a once-proud old woman padding along behind an odious nurse like an obedient child. It all comes to this."

"To Nurse Ratched I am only one more mispronounced name. To her I am Amanda Rip'er ose, not Amanda *Ri per'ous."*

The truths race on. "I am a number. Perhaps today I am number five on her list. She is anxious to be done with me so she can go on to number six."

As we near the inner door the unspeakable real truth comes to me. *"She thinks I am a bother."*

We walk through the door and I stop. Nurse Ratched goes on, then turns around to wait for me. She doesn't like waiting and gives me her best frown but now it pleases me to annoy her. As I start forward again I slow down my already dragging shuffle and make her wait longer. It is pleasantly satisfying to be a bother.

"Right here in this room," Nurse Ratched instructs crossly, eyeing me with suspicion. At first I pretend not to hear but I follow as she leads me through an open door. Like the restless man, I am tired of waiting. "Finally," I whisper to myself.

Nurse Ratched tells me where to sit. She does her eye thing, purses her lips, and gives me one last once-over. She hesitates and looks me up and down again. "She is trying to decide if I am intact," I think. She makes her decision in my favor, turns quickly, goes out the door and, with an *in your face* attitude, closes it with more noise than necessary. Her footsteps click as she walks down the long outside hall. As the clicks fade into nothing, I am left alone behind a closed door in a little cubicle of a room.

The new room is still. There are no comforting noises here; no muffled television sounds in the background, no soft rustling of papers, no quiet murmurs of people talking, no dependable ticking of a clock. A hollow lonely silence is in this room. Already, even in a few seconds, the silence rings in my ears and pounds at my aloneness with dogged persistence.

I scrunch down in my chair, listening to the silence and pondering my irrelevance. Tears well up in my eyes and slide down my cheeks, just as the sad lady's tears welled up and slid down her cheeks. I do not try to brush mine away. In this noiseless cubicle of a room where the silence is relentless and where I am all alone, it is strangely comforting to let my tears fall freely. By myself I take my time and quietly cry.

After a while the tears ebb. I feel depleted and empty and know I am finished crying. I sit still in my chair waiting for something to happen. Perhaps there will be approaching footsteps or perhaps there will be a gentle knock on the door. To mark time I count the ticks of an imaginary clock. The something I am waiting for does not happen.

I soon grow weary of counting ticks. Resigned, I sigh and settle in and contemplate filling the time space ahead. I think it will be another long wait for one **Amanda Riperos (*Ri per'ous*), an old person.**

Marty Jasper

"Loneliness is everything it is cracked up to be."

Alan Alda

Marty Runs Deep

The inside lights of the 7-Eleven are on. Seeing them from far down the highway, the warm glow is comforting. I feel like a sailor on a foggy sea who has just spotted the beacon of a familiar lighthouse.

I pull my Chevy into a parking spot near the door, turn off the engine, and sit for a while. This is my routine; park, turn off the engine, and sit by myself in my car. The next part of my routine is deciding it is time to join the world, which I will do soon. This morning it is cold. Already chilled because my car heater only works on a good day, which this day is not, I sit and shiver.

When I finally go inside Margie is working behind the counter by the cash register. Flashing her usual friendly smile she says, "You're right on time, Marty." She always greets me with the same words which are, "You're right on time, Marty." Usually I get my own paper cup for coffee but today Margie takes a cup from the stack. She turns the spigot on the big silver urn and the coffee gurgles into the cup.

"Just made it fresh. Knew you were coming," she tells me.

She opens the bakery case and, with a napkin, picks out one of the chocolate doughnuts I have with my coffee every morning. Anxious to break off chunks of the doughnut and dunk them into the coffee, I pay and head for the counter by the window. Margie and I don't talk. She has her work and I don't want to bother her. *Not that I have a lot to talk about.*

The coffee is fresh and hot, the way I like it. I lean onto the counter with my head low taking my time sipping and dunking, waiting patiently for the caffeine and the sugar to make me feel better. I hope they will shake off the heavy blanket of grogginess that weighs down on my shoulders.

Sitting at the counter sipping and dunking I watch the usual people coming and going. Today the man who wears nice suits comes in, tending to business with his phone at his ear, nodding his head as he listens. Suddenly he looks at his watch. "I'll be there in, at most, twenty minutes," he says into the phone, "and we'll take care of it then." As he puts the phone in his pocket he heads to the coffee urn. The man annoys me and I don't like him. I think he is arrogant. *Not that he cares that I think he is arrogant.* He gets his coffee and swaggers up to Margie to pay.

"You're out of here, Man," I say to myself as he heads for the door.

Watching him through the big window in front of me, I see he drives a new Lexus, parked beside my rusted-out Chevy. He looks through the side window of my Chevy and frowns and shakes his head. The man should mind his own business. I add *Nosy* and *Rude* to *Arrogant* on my **I Don't Like You** list of words.

I sit a long time with my coffee, soaking in the warmth of the room. Maybe Margie will notice my cup is almost empty. Sometimes she refills my cup and says, "Second one on the house." When she says this I treat myself to another chocolate doughnut. On this day

Margie says, "Second one on the house." She refills my cup so I buy my doughnut and go back to my perch by the window.

Yesterday James, the head of the produce department, said, "We have to talk tomorrow about how you are working out, Marty." Does he think I'm not working out? Most of the young guys in the department more or less ignore me. They talk to each other like buddies and slap each other with high-fives. They ask, "Hey, Marty, how's it going?" but after they ask they walk away.

I slow down with the coffee and doughnut because my hands are shaking. I try to keep them steady but the shaking doesn't stop and the hot coffee sloshes over the rim of the cup before I can put it down. Then I can't hold on to the cup and I drop it. The coffee spills all over the counter and a big brown blob heads for the edge. Margie sees what happened and grabs a cloth and runs over. "It's O.K.," she calls out as she is running. "I'll get it." Working quickly with her cloth she sponges up the blob. "It's not a big deal, Marty," she assures me.

I decide to leave. Quickly I pick up the empty cup and take it to the trash can by the door. Margie gives me an *are you sure?* look but doesn't try to change my mind. Instead she says, "You take care now. Have a good day, Marty. You hear?"

"Thanks, Margie, for helping me," I tell her as I head outside. Getting into my car, I look down and there is a big spot of coffee on my pants. I start my car and rev the engine and roar out of the lot.

A few miles down the highway I rummage around for my Beethoven CD, fit it into the slot, and turn the volume high. Driving across town to my doctor's office I think about James, working through all of the possible reasons he wants to talk. Now that I think about it I'm pretty sure I'm not working out. When we talk, I wonder if James will tell me my job is on the line.

The waiting room of my doctor's office is quiet when I go in, except for the talk coming from the muted television set in the corner. I find a chair and settle in. The nurse comes in several times to call for people but my name doesn't come up. For a long time I wait, getting edgier by the minute. I try talking to the woman next to me but she doesn't want to talk. *Not that I'm such a great person to talk to.* I sit by myself and work out a shortcut across town to my job.

A new couple comes in. The woman struggles to get her walker through the door while the man who is with her stands aside smirking, watching the struggle. Then the woman gets the walker caught on the side of the door. Just as I am standing up to go across the room to help and while I'm at it maybe I'll punch the guy in the nose, the woman turns the walker slightly and it eases through the door. She makes her way across the room to a chair and sits down and starts crying. The man stops at the desk to sign in and joshes with the young woman there. Smiling, he turns around and walks to the chair beside the crying woman and sits down, opening his newspaper and ignoring her.

"Marty Jasper," the nurse calls. I jump up and exclaim, "Finally!" louder than I mean to.

"Right in this room," the nurse orders in a sharp voice. I follow her and sit down on the black metal chair she points to. It is cold in the room. Pulling my jacket around me, I wish I could go back to the 7-Eleven where it is warm.

After a while there is a soft knock on the door. When the doctor comes in, on an impulse I reach out my hand and greet him in a loud high-five buddy voice. "HEY, how's it going, Doc?"

He shakes my hand and answers, "Fine, thanks."

"GLAD to hear it," I say in the same loud high-five buddy voice.

The doctor gives me a questioning look so I say, "REALLY glad to hear it," one more time, like we really are buddies.

He gives me another one of his looks. Turning around, he opens his file and lays out papers on the desk. "Let's get started here, Marty," he says.

Watching him lay out his papers, I think there are two of us in this room but only one of us feels fine, thanks, and it isn't Marty Jasper. I am cold and tired and bogged down with worry. I am sitting on a hard chair in a little square room with a doctor who is most likely going to give me unwelcome news. "Feeling rotten and who cares," is the answer to how it is going for Marty today. *Not that anybody is asking how it is going for Marty today.*

Suddenly, on another impulse, I decide what I will do. Sitting here on this hard chair in this box of a room that is cold, I know exactly what I will do. I will listen carefully to the news from the doctor. After I listen and my appointment is finished, it will not be a shortcut across town to work for Marty. No way. Not on this day. On this day Marty is going to get into his rusted-out Chevy and turn the volume up on his Beethoven and head back to the 7-Eleven. When he gets there he is going to say, "Hi, Margie, I'm back," and he will go to the big silver urn and open the spigot and the hot steaming coffee will gurgle into his cup, and he will be warm and he will sit at the counter a long time and maybe even eat another chocolate doughnut.

Again the doctor says, "Let's get started here. Let's talk serious for a few minutes, Marty." He picks up some papers from the desk and I lean in to hear the report.

I smile and think the doctor is fine, thanks, and now I am fine, thanks, too. It is a good day for me after all. Not that anyone cares that it is a good day for me.

Not that anyone cares that it is a good day for me.

Not that anyone cares . . .

Agnes Bruninski

"I know of only one duty,

and that is to love."

Albert Camus

The Price to Pay

Agnes was by herself again in the book corner. Her seatwork was finished so she went to the corner of the room where there was a rocking chair by the bookcase. Picking out a book, she slipped onto the seat of the chair to read.

Unlike many of the children in her class who liked being with others, Agnes liked spending time alone. In appearance she was somewhat different from the other girls but not glaringly different. Her dark, plain dresses didn't always fit properly but they were clean. All of the little girls wore cotton stockings under their dresses but Agnes's stockings wrinkled around her thin ankles. Her outside for recess coat was too long and it was frayed at the wrists but it was not unlike some of the other coats at recess. It is true Agnes was slightly out of sync in appearance, which might have accounted for some of her being alone, but the real reason she was alone was because she chose to be so. Open to friendship when opportunity presented itself she was a willing participant. Truthfully, though, Agnes thought the usual chattering of children her age was vapid and inane.

When she wasn't reading Agnes spent time watching the world, contemplating how things worked. She watched the children in the classroom and she watched the teacher. Sometimes her eyes roamed to the big windows at the side of the classroom where, in the spring and the fall, she watched the leaves on the trees twitter in the soft breezes. In the winter she watched ice and snow collecting on the branches of the same trees. Even though she didn't choose to enter the play; instead, spending her time reading and watching the world, it was clear to those who knew her that Agnes was contented and at ease. She was also beyond her years in maturity. One could almost say, maybe stretching it a bit, the little girl was eight going on twenty-eight.

Agnes lived with her Grandmother Inez in a small second floor shabby but clean apartment, loved dearly by the old woman and doted upon by their close immigrant friends. When the bell rang to end the school day Agnes slipped into her too long, frayed-at-the-wrists coat and walked straight home, where Grandmother Inez waited for her with an after school treat. Agnes always hoped the treat would be date-filled pinwheel cookies, fresh from the oven, and she looked forward to drinking the one cup of egg coffee she was allowed each day. Grandmother Inez had difficulty speaking English but her love for Agnes didn't need a polished language. She smiled when she heard Agnes pull the heavy downstairs door open and come bounding up the stairs, using the key on the ribbon around her neck to open the door of the apartment. Meeting her there, the old woman gathered the little girl in her arms and rubbed her back with soft gentle strokes.

Agnes learned on her own to watch her back to evade trouble and she learned to watch Grandmother Inez's back, too. The truth was, their roles switched during her growing up years. Grandmother Inez slowly failed and Agnes stepped into the role of caregiver. When the old woman began to lose her memory, Agnes remembered for her.

When Agnes came home from high school in the afternoons and slipped her key into the lock, her grandmother sat in the big chair in the living room with her eyes closed, waiting for Agnes to come and waiting for her to make their snack. When one day she came home and Grandmother Inez's eyes were closed for the last time, it was Agnes who called the doctor and it was Agnes who called their immigrant friends to come for the small graveside funeral. It was obvious to those attending the service the once quiet, serious little girl who was eight going on twenty-eight could manage very well. No longer was she the little girl they doted upon. Agnes was a clear-thinking and capable young woman.

After losing Grandmother Inez, Agnes needed to find work. Looking around, she found a housekeeper position for a family who lived across the city. The family wanted her to be a live-in, an arrangement that suited her fine as she had no desire to keep the apartment where loneliness and keen, poignant memories lurked in every corner. She sold the furnishings, kept only a few mementos, and was sad but relieved to turn the key in the lock for the last time and leave her childhood home behind. As Agnes settled into the big unfamiliar house she watched carefully to see how things were done. She threw her energy into mastering her new responsibilities. For the most part she was satisfied with her situation.

As she slowly came to terms with her grief and as her position became more secure, not surprisingly Agnes began to think about having her own home. Other girls her age were marrying. She thought there was no hurry about it but, as she went about her work, thoughts crept into her head about being married and having a home of her own. Opportunity presented itself quite by accident or, perhaps, it wasn't an accident but a perfectly-timed twist of fate leaning in her favor. One beautiful spring day when all was right with the world a young garden worker knocked on the kitchen door to report he had just now cut the water hose with the lawnmower. He was very sorry and he wished to pay for the damage. Agnes looked him over right then and didn't miss his strong muscular body and unruly dark hair that needed trimming. She asked him in for a cup of her egg coffee, just fresh, opened a tin of her date-filled pinwheel cookies, and sat at the table with him as he told her how the accident happened.

"I wasn't thinking about my work," the young man said. "I was thinking about this perfect day. Instead of paying attention to cutting the grass, I watched a robin building its nest."

Agnes listened, thinking she could teach him some things about watching. What she said aloud was, "It is good you knocked on the door to pay." What she said to herself was, "Not everyone in the world would offer to pay for a damaged water hose." Taking another look at this very handsome and seemingly honest man, she urged him to have more coffee.

As he was talking and drinking coffee and enjoying the most delicious cookies he had ever eaten, the young man took a good look at Agnes, too, and he didn't miss her nicely-rounded figure and her striking cornflower-blue eyes and her shiny blond hair done up in a heavy braid down her back. He sat back and took his time with his coffee. When he left he had a date nailed down with Agnes. Already he was thinking ahead and planning how to keep seeing this beautiful girl who had not the slightest idea of her incredible allure.

The young man knocking on the kitchen door on the beautiful spring day was Virgil Bruninski. He was seriously smitten. He definitely thought the perfectly-timed twist of fate was leaning in his favor.

It was not a twist of fate that made the forthcoming marriage a stellar union. Agnes and Virgil were mature, hard-working young people. The couple worked at the marriage and they worked at getting ahead in life. Agnes watched for opportunities and Virgil, smart and aggressive, carefully took advantage of them. To people who knew them it was not a surprise that Virgil and Agnes opened their own garden and landscaping store and, in a few years, expanded the single store into a company of several stores. Life was good for Agnes, once the quiet, serious little girl who was eight going on twenty-eight.

Today, though, sitting in the doctor's waiting room, life was not good for Agnes. The stellar marriage took a nasty turn and the years of satisfying work were over. Today she was tired and she was sick. Her thoughts went to Grandmother Inez. "I am almost as old as Grandmother when I found her in her chair," Agnes thought.

Seeing a doctor was not something Agnes wanted to do but she was alone now and she needed to be well. For a year now Virgil's home was the Alzheimer's wing of St. Luke's. She didn't want to leave him there alone and she wanted to see him every day, even if he didn't remember she was Agnes, his wife.

The truth was, Virgil didn't remember much of anything. Earlier on, when it was clear he was losing his memory they sold the business, but now Virgil didn't remember the sale. "Are the maple trees selling well?" he asked one day. During the Christmas season he wondered, "Did the poinsettias come in yet?"

When the questions came Agnes smiled and assured him with, "Oh, Virgil, everything is going fine. Don't worry about a thing." Then she gathered him in her arms and rubbed his back with soft gentle strokes.

As Agnes waited for her name to be called she watched people coming into the waiting room. She watched the nurse open the inner door and come into the room carrying her files, scowling as she called names.

When it was Agnes's time the nurse looked at the green file in her hand and called, "Brouniski." Taking a second look at the name she called it again. "Agnes Brouniski," she called loudly. This time she scanned the room, looking for Agnes.

Agnes stood up. In a clear voice she corrected the pronunciation of her name. *"Broo nin' ski,"* she said proudly. "My name is *Broo nin' ski*, not Brou nis' ki."

Agnes noticed the nurse didn't acknowledge her name was pronounced, *"Broo nin' ski."* She couldn't miss the nurse choosing to ignore the correction. Quickly, from habit, she reminded herself to watch her back.

On this day, though, Agnes was tired. She felt the sickness come washing over her. It was the huge wave of sickness, showing up without warning whenever it felt like it. It always crashed in at first with surprising force before quieting down to stay awhile and sending out little ripples of pain. Wanting to sit down again, Agnes wondered if she had the strength on this day to watch her back and, if she didn't have the strength, would it make any difference? Yesterday Virgil called her Clara, his youngest sister, and the day before yesterday he thought Agnes was the nurse. Sometimes he thanked Agnes for her business at the store.

Agnes wondered what would be coming next for Virgil. She wondered what would be coming next for her in the doctor's patient room and she wondered what would be coming for her later when she left the doctor's office.

Agnes, once the quiet serious little girl who was eight going on twenty-eight and Agnes, once the loving caregiver for Grandmother Inez and now Agnes, the loving caregiver for Virgil, with practiced habit pulled her back straight. By herself, all alone, **Agnes Bruninski (pronounced *Broo nin'ski*), walked behind the nurse and steeled herself for the uncertain future.**

Ann and Matthew Jordon

"No one ever told me that

grief felt so like fear."

C. S. Lewis

On the Corner

of Living and Dying

When I was in high school a beautiful girl moved to our town. She came at the beginning of my senior year when her family built a new home on the outskirts of town.

The new girl caught my attention. Not only was she beautiful but she had a fascinating way about her. Every morning I watched her walk past my house on her way to school. I was enamored with her light step and the toss of her head as she turned the corner. She more or less floated like a carefree spirit, but she was anything but a floating carefree spirit. I could see right away the girl knew exactly where she was going and what she intended to do with her day. The light step and the toss of her head were extras she threw in for challenge. They clearly announced to the world, "Get on with you. Don't push me around. I have your number."

We started walking to school together. During my last year and her next-to-last year of school we spent much of our time with each other. I was a serious young man with lofty goals. I talked my heart out to the girl, sharing my dreams for the future. She listened, pulling me into her heart and bringing a light touch to my too-serious life. I was pretty sure I would have a hard time living without this girl and found myself making plans to spend my life with her.

We were married the summer after her graduation when I was twenty and she was barely eighteen. My promise to her was undying admiration and fierce loyalty. To my credit, I always kept my promise. Her promise to me was to always and forever keep her light step. She added, at my insistence, "I will float like a carefree spirit," assuring me airily her promise would be kept. I remember her exact words. "Not to worry, Matthew. It is the way I am."

"Matthew, look." Ann interrupts my thoughts in a quiet whisper. I lean in to hear. "Matthew, look at the nurse. What do you think?"

I look, and see a stocky, middle-aged nurse scowling at her approaching patient; an old woman saying something about how to pronounce her name. The nurse doesn't respond, quickly backs through the open door behind her, and the old woman follows.

"I think the nurse looks pretty ornery," I say quietly. The *ornery* word makes us both smile. Then my lips go thin. My Ann is somewhere on the patient list and I don't want the nurse to even think about being ornery to her. Ann sees the change in my smile and gives me a little jab; a jab to remind me of the agreement we made together. It is an agreement I am determined to keep.

Waiting: A Collective

We found out two weeks ago my Ann is dying.

She sat at the table that day with a cup of tea in front of her, waiting for me to come home. "What's up?" I asked.

"I need to tell you something," Ann said. Her face was twisted in a strange kind of way. My stomach knotted. This was Ann's morning to see her doctor. There were some tests. The doctor called them *routine tests*. "Go on to your meeting," Ann insisted. "No need for you to miss it."

So when I came back from my meeting Ann told me what she needed to tell me. She sat scrunched down in her chair and wouldn't look me in the eye. As her body shook, as she fought back tears, she told me in a very small voice the news I could hardly bear then and is inconceivable to me now. It was the worst news of my entire life.

Ann sat at the table that day and told me she would be dying.

She sat up tall in her chair and looked at me straight, her eyes clouding with the tears she couldn't hold back. This time, in a loud voice, she blurted out the next worst news of my entire life. "Possibly as soon as six months from now," she said.

I held out my arms and Ann fell into them. My eyes filled with tears, too, and there the two of us sat. We sat there hanging on to each other, stunned, not believing this could happen. In just a few seconds the death sentence permeated all of the space around us, seeping in and oozing with brutal hatefulness. It was unspeakably ugly. The longer we sat and the more we talked, the uglier it became.

Our talk was riddled with questions and punctured with stabs of a reality we didn't want. Mixed in with the questions and stabs were long periods of unbelieving silence. We wondered if the doctor could be wrong about the dying, desperately wanting to grab on to any thread of hope. We asked ourselves how this could have come to be. We chastised ourselves for not reading the signs or, at the very least, for not having suspicions. Ann said there would be pain and we both cried when we thought about her hurting. The talk and the long silences went on for a long time. We were caught in a time warp of our own and we couldn't get ourselves back into the real world.

We were paralyzed with fear.

Ann said, "I'm so tired." I gathered her in my arms and helped her to our bed, pulling the blankets around us and holding her close. We slept in a deep bottomless chasm, blocking out the world, hoping we would not wake up, ever.

Later Ann said, "I've been thinking, Matthew. We could have some time together, just the two of us."

"Yes," I said. "We could do that." Knowing Ann, I was pretty sure she already had the framework of a plan squared away in her head. I was also pretty sure her plan would be how we would do it because this is the way things work with Ann.

"We could pretend for a while," she said. "For a few weeks, maybe three, we could shut out the world." She went on. "We would not tell anyone about me dying. We would live in a little cocoon of safety, laughing and smiling and remembering the good times." Now Ann was choosing her words carefully, working out the details of her plan as she talked. "It would be just the two of us who know about what we are doing," she said again.

There was more to come but right away, when Ann was talking, I knew I would do the pretending. I was willing to do anything to keep, for a little while longer, the life with Ann that I love. I was sure I could keep my panic in check for three weeks. If it meant pretending like a grinning idiot for Ann's last weeks without pain, so be it.

For two weeks now we have been playing the pretend game and I am proud to say I have not failed Ann in keeping it going. She doesn't know I am also deeply into a desperate tug-of-war with God. Daily, as I struggle with my end of the rope, I cry out to him in pain. I beg to him on my knees for Ann's life and I have offered him every bargaining chip I can think of. When I look at Ann, though, and see her failing, I know I am not winning. I am not even close. God has a firm grip on the rope. He is holding his ground and he is steadily taking mine.

We watch a new couple come into the waiting room. The man comes in first and the woman follows. She struggles at the door, trying to manage her walker by herself. With a smirk on his face the man stands and watches the struggle. Ann and I don't go to help the woman and no one else goes to help her. We all watch the uncomfortable scene from our chairs. I don't know why one of us doesn't stand up and walk to the door to give the woman some help.

When she finally gets her walker into the room the woman slowly inches across the room to a chair, turns around and sits down, and starts to cry. The man ignores her as he stops at the intake counter, smiling at the girl there and chatting with her. All during this time I see he is very happy. His disgusting display of happiness makes me furious. How dare he be happy? He has no right to be happy. This poor excuse for a man can't be happy if his wife is not happy.

Ann looks at my contorted face and jabs me again.

I sit back and take stock, listing one-by-one the way things are. The list isn't good. I am sitting in a doctor's waiting room with my wife who is going to die. I am pretending to be a happy person. I am watching an ornery nurse scowl at everyone she calls. I am glued to my chair, not even able to get up to help a needy old woman. I am mad as hell at a man I've never seen before.

I am scared and try to think rationally.

The truth is, I am backed against a wall with this terrible situation. I can't say, "This, too, shall pass." This terrible situation is not going to pass. Every day it is going to get worse and then finally, at the end, it is going to crush me into the wall with brute force and I am going to cry out in pain and anger, "Foul! Damn it! Foul!"

Ann links her arm through mine. She smiles at me and puts her head on my shoulder. The room is quiet. I hear the loud steady ticking of the wall clock and think we have been here a long time and we should be called soon. Then I think the clock is ticking away the minutes and the hours and the days and the weeks to Ann's death.

In misery, I blink back tears. I put my arm around Ann and pull her close. **With great effort I put on my idiot grin and resolve to keep it plastered on my face.**

Rose Middleton

"There comes a time when the risk to remain tight in the bud is more painful than the risk it took to blossom."

Anais Nin

Fierce Bad Rat

"I am Rose, and this is my story."

It is a story I'm not proud to tell, except for the happy ending. Really, though, who is to say it has a happy ending. The memories of abuse are anything but happy and they don't go away. The memories hide in little spots in your head and jump out to scare you when you least expect them to and, if that isn't enough to make you feel bad, the remnants of shame have a way of hanging around to keep your happiness in check.

No, this is not a story to be proud of. The only proud I feel is of the people who helped me in the doctor's office on the day of my appointment.

There is trouble getting my walker through the door of the waiting room. I finally yank it hard and it slips through. I head for two empty chairs and carefully sit down on one of them and put my purse on my walker. Then the tears start. I try to blink them back. As they stream down my face I brush them away. The tears keep coming. There is nothing to do but let them have their way.

The people waiting in the room watch me cry, guardedly keeping track from over the tops of their newspapers and magazines. "She is an old woman who has lived her life," they think. "Now she is at the end of her road and it is time for her to check out. It is too bad for her." When they see how sad I am and how I can't stop crying they are embarrassed for me and thoughtfully look down.

They are right about one thing. It is true I am at the end of my road, but it isn't the end of the winding down old-age road they are thinking about. My road of abuse isn't winding down. It is getting longer and I see no end to it. My road has ruts of hatefulness and disrespect. It is pocked with deep camouflaged holes of lies and disappointments that cruelly and deceitfully steal my dignity and my pride. My road makes me tired. Walking on it drains my strength.

Most of the people in the waiting room tire of watching me but sitting across the room is a woman whose eyes keep coming back. This woman holds herself apart from the rest of us and waits like a lady for her appointment. She is dressed nicer than most of us. She sits straight and tall on her chair and I like the way she holds her head high. Her steely eyes do not give one hint of a smile. Two people by the wall aren't shy about watching me either. The man and the woman sit by themselves, holding hands and smiling.

Here comes Ray, prancing across the room to sit beside me on the empty chair. I am an expert at knowing what Ray is thinking. Right now he is thinking, "Rose is crying. Again. She always cries. What an embarrassment this woman is."

Ray, the *prancer*. Ray, the *lover boy*. Ray, the *abuser*.

My *husband*, Ray.

This morning, without warning, Ray kicked me. I was alone at the kitchen table with my second cup of coffee, thinking about this doctor appointment I am nervous about and making a plan in my head for how to manage it. Ray came in with a scowl on his face. He growled, "Where is my jacket? I need it to take you to that doctor today." He walked over and gave me a hard kick on the leg, then turned around and strutted out of the room. This is what he does. In addition to his ugly tantrums with me ending up on the floor he does dirty little kicks and hits. When he leaves I don't know if he will be coming back to give me more.

"In your face, *Ray*. Find your own jacket, *Ray*," is what I thought as I sat there on edge waiting to see if he would come back.

When I finally get my tears under control I sneak some peeks at my lady, liking again how she holds her head high. With her clear skin and her nice clothes, she is pretty. "I could be pretty," I think. "Even with my walker, I could be pretty. . ." At the edges of my mind I allow myself some thinking about being pretty.

"Hello, there." I look up, startled. It is the woman from the happy-looking couple, standing by my chair.

"Hello," I answer, barely whispering. In shame, I look down at my lap to hide my swollen tear-stained face, hoping this woman will not dwell on it and hoping that please, dear God, she will go away. As sure as the world turns she is going to ask me why I am crying and if she can help.

"Come and sit with Matthew and me," the woman says. Just like that she says it. She doesn't say, "I notice you aren't feeling well," or "Can I help?" She only says, "Come and sit with Matthew and me."

"Rose is with me," growls *instantly alert* Ray. "She is doing fine now."

The woman ignores Ray. "My name is Ann and I want you to sit with me," she says again. "There is an empty chair beside me. I want you to sit there."

Ray doesn't like it. "I told you she is with me. It's hard for her to move."

The woman who is Ann keeps her eyes on me and acts like Ray isn't sitting beside me. I think she is playing *Harvey*. You know the game. If can't see him and I can't hear him, he must not be here.

"Please come with me," she repeats in a soft friendly voice, like she is talking to her best friend.

The woman doesn't hear Ray's protest when he stands up and angrily sputters, "Rose can't go." Still playing the *Harvey* game, she looks straight at me and I feel her eyes boring into me as she waits for my answer.

I know what I want to do. I know exactly what I want to do. I reach for my walker and lean on it to get up from my chair. I want to sit on the chair beside this woman who calls herself Ann, who is with the man she calls Matthew, and I intend to do it. We start walking, slowly making our way across the room, Ann leading the way. When we get to her side of the room I turn my walker around and sit down on the chair she points to, making sure not to look back at Ray. I do look across the room to find my lady. If she happened to smile I would give her a 'thumbs up' and smile back, but she is not in her chair.

Ann looks at Matthew and nods her head and Matthew puts out his hand and pats her arm. They don't talk and I don't say anything either.

The nurse opens the inner door with her stack of files. I see her glance at Ray, sitting alone, glowering like a spoiled child. Looking across the room she sees me sitting with Ann and Matthew. Her eyes go back to Ray and narrow, something like how a cat narrows its eyes when it spies a rat. When a cat spies a rat it stops in its tracks and doesn't move. It narrows its eyes and readies for the pounce. This is how the nurse is acting. She is acting like a cat that spies a rat.

The room is still and I am suddenly afraid. The wall clock scolds me with its loud steady ticking, relentlessly beating out my name. *"Do you hear me, ROSE? What are you doing here, ROSE?"* The scolding won't stop. *"You should go home, ROSE . . . ROSE . . . ROSE . . ."*

The cat moves. Looking at one of the files she breaks the silence, stopping the clock's hateful lashing out. She meows out loudly, "Ann Jordan, please."

Ann, who is *Ann Jordan* now, and Matthew look at each other. They look at the cat nurse and they look at me but they don't get up. The cat nurse purses her lips, looks down, and her paws quickly flip through the other files she is carrying. Opening one of them, glancing at the first page, she meows out clearly, "I am also calling Rose Middleton."

Rose Middleton! I am Rose Middleton! This cat means Rose Middleton should come along with Ann Jordan and Matthew. She meowed out my name. She wants me to come.

My heart is pounding. I put my hands on my walker and Matthew is right there helping me get up. Ann Jordon mouths, "Yes," at the cat nurse and the cat nurse looks back at her and nods. As sure as the world turns, I see her lick her whiskers as she watches me make my way across the room, with Ann and Matthew following.

Instantly Alert is beside us. "I'll be coming with my wife," he tells the cat nurse in a shrill bully voice that sounds very much like the high squeak of a rat. Glaring at me he squeaks again, "She's with me."

Skillfully, Matthew steps between us to block Ray's way. Ann Jordan steps up and puts her arm around me. "Keep walking, Rose." she whispers. "Just keep walking."

Taking in the scene before her, Cat turns to Ray and meows out with loud authority, "The doctor will see Rose alone today. You are not to come. Please wait in the Waiting Room." Her eyes narrow again as she warns Ray to back off. Pulling herself to her full height she arches her back and hisses out a repeat order; an order not to be defied. **"You will not be coming, Mr. Middleton."**

Mr. Rat Middleton is surprised. He looks around and sees he is outnumbered. Calculating his odds he immediately knows he is at a disadvantage. Mr. Rat Middleton puts out his lip to show two sharp teeth. His little beady rat eyes lash out at the nurse with contempt. He turns to me and narrows his eyes. Hatred shoots out of them in little piercing daggers. Taking his time, he arrogantly tosses his pointed head, shrugs, and slinks back to his chair. Watching in amazement I see a long, heavy tail dragging along behind, swishing from one side to the other in perfect rhythm.

Ann still has her arm around me as the three of us approach the inner door. "Thank you, Ann," I say.

"Shall I come with you to see the doctor?" she asks as she puts her hand over mine on the walker. "I'll be glad to come."

"We're coming with you," Matthew announces. "We've just decided," he tells me as he looks at Ann for confirmation. Still looking at Ann he adds, with a catch in his throat, "We have lots of time, you know. This is a special day for us." Then both Ann and Matthew do something I don't understand. They both burst into tears.

The cat leads me to a room and Ann and Matthew follow. "This will be your room," Cat says with a new soft soothing meow. She reaches out her paw to touch my shoulder gently. "The doctor will be here soon." Her unblinking eyes are steady when she adds, "I'll be back, too, and we'll talk." As sure as the world turns there is a soft purring sound as she goes out into the hall and softly closes the door behind her.

The woman named Ann Jordan and the man named Matthew sit with me in the room and we are together again without talking. We wait in the silence for a long time.

When a knock finally comes and the door opens it is the doctor in his white coat, smiling at me. Right behind him is the nurse. Looking straight at me she says in the new soft voice, "I told you I would be back."

"Let's get down to business here," the doctor says.

I sit slumped in my chair and know what I have to do but I am frightened and embarrassed and ashamed. I cast about for words to begin and tentatively make the start in the best way I can. Looking at the doctor, then looking down at my lap, I manage to whisper softly, "I need to talk to someone about what is happening to me."

The doctor tilts his head and looks at me curiously. "Yes?" he says. "Go on, please." When he tells me, "Go on, please," it is my green light to go ahead. I draw in my breath. I begin saying what I came to say.

The doctor listens and the nurse and Ann Jordan and Matthew listen. Ann is close beside me, reaching out her arms to hold me, and the nurse is in front of me. She is on her knees, holding my hands with tears in her eyes, nodding for me to go on as the doctor asks me question after question. It isn't easy. I struggle but I talk truthfully, wincing as the words come out. In all the years of misery they are words not heard by one person. Now, as I struggle to say them, I am amazed four people in the room all want to hear what I have to say.

There is so much shame. It is hard to look the doctor in the eye when I answer his questions. The relief of sharing my burden should take away some of the shame but it doesn't. I am wading up to my neck in shame. The water is thick and dirty.

When I stop talking and sit still for a minute, I remember my pretty lady in the Waiting Room. It is hard to forget her steely unsmiling eyes. I wonder what she would think if she were here. I decide to sit up tall on my chair with my back straight, and I try getting my chin up. It feels good to hold my head high.

In a tearful outburst I blurt out, "This is a special day for me, too. I think this is the first day of a new life for me." A surprised quiet follows my outburst. Suddenly, in the quiet, Matthew and Ann grab each other and hold on for dear life, *like there is no tomorrow.* The doctor steps back and smiles and nods his head and the nurse reaches out her hand to gently pat my shoulder. Right then I know for sure I am in good hands. Right then I know I can stop my talk.

This story doesn't end in the doctor's office. When I said in the tearful outburst, "I think this is the first day of a new life for me," I said it right. When I left the doctor's office that day in the care of others, things took a solid turn for the better. I do have a new life. As I said before, though, the memories of the years of abuse are staying with me. They show up at unexpected times and they always scare me. No matter how many times I bury the memories away for good they have a cruel way of popping up. It is true, too. The remnants of shame stubbornly hang around.

I said at the beginning and now again at the end, **"I am Rose, and this is my story."** It is my story about what happened in the doctor's waiting room and in his patient room, told as truthfully as I can remember. *As sure as the world turns,* ***it is the way it was.***

"All human wisdom is summed up in two words; wait and hope."

Alexandre Dumas,
the Elder

Appendix

The Older Population

The older population of persons 65 or older, in 2011, represented 13.3% of the United States population. This is over one in every eight Americans.

The number of Americans aged 45 – 64 who will reach 65 over the next two decades increased by 33% from 2000 to 2011.

There were 53,364 persons aged 100 or more in 2010 (0.13% of the total 64+ population). This is a 65% increase from the 1980 figure of 32,194.

Information based on online data from
the U. S. Census Bureau.

Discussion Questions

1. *Nurse Ratched* appears in the first stories as cross, insensitive, and ornery. Why does she have a change of heart in Rosa's story?

2. In what ways does Marty *run deep*, as the title of his story suggests? What clues tell us he is sensitive and caring? Do you know a *Marty?* How common are *Marty's*?

3. Discuss the struggles of losing a spouse to death. What emotions can manifest themselves at this sad time?

4. Several people in the waiting room watched Rose cry but, for various reasons, did not offer comfort. Should they have offered comfort? Why or why not? Does it surprise you it was Anne who approached Rose?

5. In our older population, how prevalent is the feeling of irrelevance?

6. Agnes is unsure if she makes a difference in Virgil's life. Can/Does a caregiver make a difference in the life of an Alzheimer's patient? What suggestions do you have for a caregiver?

7. Discuss medical waiting rooms. Are there ways to make waiting rooms more comfortable for the people who spend time in them? What would an ideal waiting room look like, feel like, be like?

8. Is there a character you especially care for? Why?

9. It has been said, *"Being old is not for sissies."* Do you agree? "**Waiting: a Collective**" deals with issues of the elderly. What are other issues?

10. Who would benefit from reading this book?

11. Mother Teresa says, *"I am concerned about your neighbor. Do you know your next-door neighbor?"* Does reading "**Waiting: a Collective**" make her quote more meaningful?

. . . *about the author*

Virginia Sievers, author of ***"Waiting: a Collective"***, feels deeply about her characters. Her readers also become endeared to them, finding them unforgettable. They return often to reread the stories, awakening emotions felt at the first reading.

Virginia lives in Minnesota and Arizona. She loves gardening, reading, and writing.

She holds a Master's Degree from the University of Minnesota.

. . . about Carl

and All You Can Eat Books, Inc.

Virginia Sievers thanks Carl Sievers for encouraging her to write ***"Waiting: a Collective"*** and ***"No Dancing in the Kitchen: a Collective"***, and for editing and formatting the books. She also thanks him for the cover designs.

The author is grateful to ***All You Can Eat Books, Inc.*** for publishing her books.

All You Can Eat Books, Inc. welcomes comments about

"Waiting: a Collective"

Address comments to:

All You Can Eat Books, Inc.

9491 Foxford Road

Chanhassen, MN 55317

or contact

elainesievers@hotmail.com

22416957R10049

Made in the USA
San Bernardino, CA
06 July 2015